Dear Parents and Educators,

Welcome to Penguin Young Readers! As parents and educators, you know that each child develops at his or her own pace—in terms of speech, critical thinking, and, of course, reading. Penguin Young Readers recognizes this fact. As a result, each Penguin Young Readers book is assigned a traditional easy-to-read level (1–4) as well as a Guided Reading Level (A–P). Both of these systems will help you choose the right book for your child. Please refer to the back of each book for specific leveling information. Penguin Young Readers features esteemed authors and illustrators, stories about favorite characters, fascinating nonfiction, and more!

Pearl and Wagner: Five Days Till Summer

LEVEL **3**

GUIDED READING LEVEL **K**

This book is perfect for a **Transitional Reader** who:
- can read multisyllable and compound words;
- can read words with prefixes and suffixes;
- is able to identify story elements (beginning, middle, end, plot, setting, characters, problem, solution); and
- can understand different points of view.

Here are some **activities** you can do during and after reading this book:
- Comprehension: Answer the following questions about the story.
  - Why did Ms. Star take her class to visit Mr. Hat's class?
  - What did Pearl think when she first saw Ms. Bean?
  - What were two ways in which Pearl described Ms. Bean to her classmates?
  - When did Pearl's opinion of Ms. Bean change and why?
- Discuss with the child how it can be wrong to "judge a book by its cover," or to jump to conclusions about someone without really knowing that person. Talk about how Pearl's initial reaction to Ms. Bean caused her to make up stories about the teacher.

Remember, sharing the love of reading with a child is the best gift you can give!

—Bonnie Bader, EdM
  Penguin Young Readers program

*Penguin Young Readers are leveled by independent reviewers applying the standards developed by Irene Fountas and Gay Su Pinnell in *Matching Books to Readers: Using Leveled Books in Guided Reading*, Heinemann, 1999.

To everyone in Mrs. Beatrice Murphy's second-grade class at Mendell Elementary, Roxbury, MA: John, Danazia, Destiny, Aliza, LaKeisha, Natalie, Kares, Angel, Edelis, Avianny, Kelvin, Miguel, Ismail, Michelle, Carlaluz, James, Chancellor, Nomaris, Zariah, Míkai, and to their terrific student teacher, Ms. Krista Paul.
—K.M.

For George and Tommy, my pals of summer —R.W.A.

Penguin Young Readers
A division of Penguin Young Readers Group
Published by The Penguin Group Penguin Group (USA) Inc., 375 Hudson Street, New York, NY 10014, U.S.A.
Penguin Group (Canada), 90 Eglinton Avenue East, Suite 700, Toronto, Ontario, Canada
M4P 2Y3 (a division of Pearson Penguin Canada Inc.)
Penguin Books Ltd, 80 Strand, London WC2R 0RL, England
Penguin Ireland, 25 St. Stephen's Green, Dublin 2, Ireland (a division of Penguin Books Ltd)
Penguin Group (Australia), 250 Camberwell Road, Camberwell, Victoria 3124, Australia
(a division of Pearson Australia Group Pty Ltd)
Penguin Books India Pvt Ltd, 11 Community Centre, Panchsheel Park, New Delhi - 110 017, India
Penguin Group (NZ), 67 Apollo Drive, Rosedale, Auckland 0632, New Zealand
(a division of Pearson New Zealand Ltd)
Penguin Books (South Africa) (Pty) Ltd, 24 Sturdee Avenue,
Rosebank, Johannesburg 2196, South Africa

Penguin Books Ltd, Registered Offices: 80 Strand, London WC2R 0RL, England

The art was created using pen and ink, watercolor, and a few colored pencils on Strathmore Bristol.

Text copyright © 2012 by Kate McMullan. Illustrations copyright © 2012 by R. W. Alley. All rights reserved.
Published in 2012 by Penguin Young Readers, an imprint of Penguin Group (USA) Inc.,
345 Hudson Street, New York, New York, 10014.
Manufactured in China.
Library of Congress Cataloging-in-Publication Data available upon request.
The publisher does not have any control over and does not assume any responsibility for
author or third-party websites or their content.
1 3 5 7 9 10 8 6 4 2
ISBN 978-0-8037-3589-7

Pearl and Wagner
Five Days Till Summer

by Kate McMullan
illustrated by R.W. Alley

Penguin Young Readers
An Imprint of Penguin Group (USA) Inc.

Contents

Chapter 1
Ants on a Log

On Monday, Henry said,

"Only five more days of school."

"Then, summer!" said Wagner.

"I can't wait," said Pearl.

"Clear your desks!" said Ms. Star.

"Not another test!" said Wagner.

"No," said Ms. Star.

"We are going to visit Mr. Hat's class.
His students will be in my class next
year.

Shall we take them a snack?"

Everybody said, "Yes!"

"Wait, Ms. Star!" said Pearl.

"Who will be *our* teacher?"

"Ms. Bean," said Ms. Star.

"Everybody wash your hands!

We're going to make Ants on a Log."

Ms. Star put out celery, cream cheese, and raisins.

Pearl and Wagner spread cream cheese on celery logs.

"Have you ever seen Ms. Bean?" Pearl asked.

"Nope," said Wagner.

"Me neither," said Henry.

He lined up raisins on the cream cheese.

"The ants go marching one by one!"

he sang.

On the way to Mr. Hat's classroom,
Pearl wondered about Ms. Bean.
Was she as nice as Ms. Star?

She passed a door with a sign beside it.

The sign said:

"Ms. Bean."

The door was open a crack.

Pearl peeked inside.

The room was quiet.

Very quiet.

Everybody was writing.

Ms. Bean walked from desk to desk.

Ms. Bean wore a green dress and floppy
brown shoes.

She was not smiling.

Nobody was smiling.

Pearl turned and ran to Mr. Hat's
room.

"We made a robot," Wagner
was telling Mr. Hat's class.
"Right, Pearl?"
"We did?" said Pearl.
She was thinking
about Ms. Bean.

"I made an electric potato,"

 said Henry.

"Wow!" said Mr. Hat's class.

"We had a dance contest," said Lulu.

"Bud and Pearl won first prize."

"We did?" said Pearl.

 She had Ms. Bean on the brain!

When it was time to go, Ms. Star waved. "See you next fall!" she said.

"I saw Ms. Bean," Pearl told Wagner
   as they walked back to their room.
"What does she look like?"
   asked Wagner.
"She looks like a bean," said Pearl.
"A mean green bean."

Chapter 2
Ms. Bean Is Mean

Pearl and Wagner walked to school
together on Tuesday.

Pearl said, "I bet Ms. Bean makes us
do a hundred jumping jacks every day."

"Why would she do *that*?" said Wagner.

"To be mean," said Pearl.

At recess, Pearl told Lulu about
Ms. Bean.

"I bet she gives spelling tests
with hard, hard words,"
she said.

"Words like 'stupendous' and
'astonishing.'"

Lulu gasped. "No!"

Pearl worked with Henry at math time.
"I bet Ms. Bean makes us count
backward from a hundred
by sevens," she said.
"Sevens?" said Henry.
"Even *I* can't do that!"

Pearl walked to the cafeteria
with Bud.

"I bet Ms. Bean talks and talks
until we miss lunch," she told him.

"Don't even *say* that!" said Bud.

After lunch, Ms. Star sat down
to read a story.
"Ms. Star!" said Lulu. "Can we be
in your class again next year?"

"Can we?" called Bud.

"Please?" said Henry.

"We're begging you!" said Wagner.

"What's all this about?" asked Ms. Star.

Everybody said, "Ms. Bean is mean!"

"My stars!" said Ms. Star.

"Who told you that?"

And everybody said, "Pearl."

"Ms. Bean and her class are coming to see us tomorrow," said Ms. Star. "After that, we can talk about whose class you want to be in next year."

"Your class, Ms. Star," said Pearl. "Your class!"

Chapter 3
THWACK!

On Wednesday, Pearl's tummy hurt.
She did not want to see the
mean green bean.
But at ten o'clock, Ms. Bean and
her class showed up.

"On Book Character Day, we all
dressed up," a boy told
Ms. Star's class.
"Even Ms. Bean. She was Pippi
Longstocking."

"Wow!" said Ms. Star's class.

"We brought you a snack we grew
in our garden," said a boy.

"Carrots and green beans with
red pepper dip," said a girl.

"Have a bean," said a boy.

"No thanks," said Pearl.

"Any questions?" said Ms. Bean.
"Will you make us do a hundred
    jumping jacks?" asked Wagner.
"Never!" said Ms. Bean.

"Will we have a spelling test
with 'stupendous' and 'astonishing'?"
asked Lulu.

"Not a chance," said Ms. Bean.

"Will you make sure we get to lunch
on time?" asked Bud.

"Every day!" said Ms. Bean.

"Will you make us count backward
from a hundred by sevens?"
asked Henry.

"Sevens?" said Ms. Bean.

"Even *I* can't do that!"

At last Ms. Bean said,

"See you next fall!"

"Not me," Pearl said softly.

"I still think Ms. Bean looks mean."

"What about Book Character Day, Pearl?"
Wagner said.

"You like to dress up."

"Not that much," said Pearl.

"What about growing a garden?"
said Wagner.

"Too many weeds," said Pearl.

"Ms. Bean's class sounds like fun to me," said Wagner.

"But nothing will be any fun without you, Pearl."

The big Student-Teacher Softball
Game was on Thursday.
Pearl, Wagner, and Henry sat
together in the stands.
Ms. Star was first up to bat.

Lulu pitched the ball.
Ms. Star hit a pop fly right to Bud.
"Nice try, Ms. Star!" called Pearl.

Ms. Bean stepped up to the plate.

Lulu threw a pitch.

THWACK!

Ms. Bean hit it over the fence.

"Stupendous!" shouted Henry.

"Astonishing!" shouted Wagner.

Ms. Bean smiled as she ran around
the bases.

She waved at everyone.

Pearl waved back.

"Hey, Wags?" she said.

"You think she can teach us to do
that?"

Friday was the last day of school.

Ms. Star brought in cupcakes.

"I baked them myself," she said.

"We will miss you next year, Ms. Star,"
said Wagner.

"We will!" said Pearl.

"So you're going to Ms. Bean's class
 after all, Pearl?" asked Ms. Star.
"That's right," said Pearl.
"But don't worry, Ms. Star.
 I will come back to visit you all the time."
"I will always be happy to see you,
 Pearl," said Ms. Star.

The bell rang and they all ran
outside into summer.
"Only seventy-two days till fall,"
said Henry.
"Then, back to school," said Wagner.
"I can't wait!" said Pearl.